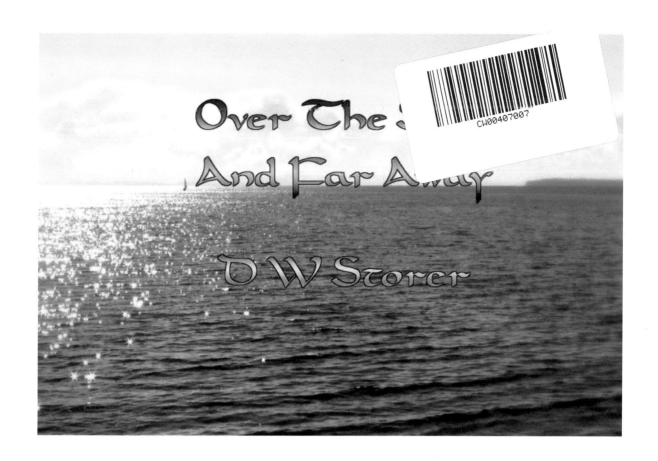

Over The Seas and Far Away

Poetry
For lovers

D W Storer

For

'S'

Worshipped as a goddess
From afar
Like the Elven
Evenstar

For Janet –

Thank you for all the
support, help, & advice –
& especially for being
my friend

With Thanks To

To my friends who have always been there to support me
As well as listening to my ramblings

Leighann Parker, Janet D. B. Heaton-Ferguson
Tie Soliwoda, Michelle Alder, Suze Johnstone
Sue Walkusky, Robin Hollifield, Sheila Shailes
Liz Rehard, Kat Morrow-Hughes, Jacqui Hodges
Debi Richens, Liz Rehard, Carole Walters, Lynda Potter

'Tis upon a lighter note I write
With a heart now free of care
For I would not have thus survived
Without all of you out there

You are across the seas and far away
And there are words that I would say
If you were here with me today
But you're across the seas and far away

Across the seas and far away
Still in my dreams you dance and play
So I must wait here for that day
Until I can those words then say

Fate over us she does hold sway
She means for us to meet one day
You are there, here I remain
Across the seas and far away

Across the seas and far away
Still in my dreams you dance and play
So I must wait here for that day
Until I can those words then say

Sat staring out across the bay
Come sun or rain, both night and day
My heart commands and I obey
Though you are so far away

Across the seas and far away
Still in my dreams you dance and play
So I must wait here for that day
Until I can those words then say

I am a moth

Drawn to your flame

For even the

Sound of your name

Eases my soul

Frees me from pain

I am a moth

Drawn to your flame

I did not sleep

Yet I did dream

Of you dancing

Through moonbeams

Singing songs

Of what might be

If you were here

Today with me

Lost in thought
I walked alone
From the shore
To return home
The sun rode low
Shadows lengthened
Hopeful I
Of Fate's intention
Heart on sleeve
In dreams caught
Of the love
That I have sought
As streetlight halos
Told of a day
When together we
Could walk this way

Your eyes are like

A lightning strike

And how they set

My soul alight

To feel the touch of your hand
To hear you softly breathing
Would give rise to the question
Is this real, or am I dreaming?

To simply walk beside you
To see the smile within your eyes
To hear you when you speak
To hear you gently sigh

To hold you close so tightly
To act the fool and make you laugh
To watch the world go by together
That is my hopeful path

To be there when you wake
And before you go to sleep
For you to know I'm there
By the sound of my heart beat

As eventide
Gives way to night
As the sun
Does ride so low
The stars and moon
Will show in dreams
Where my soul will go
And 'tis to you
That I must come
Even if 'tis but in sleep
For the visions of
Such halcyon days
Alas,
They are too brief

A whisper of

Love and devotion

Is what keeps

Our world in motion

Forgive me if I seem a fool
Wondering why life can be cruel
But you give me hope when I need it most
What if we'd met all those years ago
Where we'd be now we cannot know
But maybe Fate would have been kind?

If we had met even yesterday
In this imperfect world
Would we have learned to fly?
If I knew of some magic word
I'd surely say it every day
As long as I'm alive

Some might say I'm naïve
Since I strive so to believe
But you give me hope when I need it most
If knew then what I now know
Things would be different- don't ask me how
I'd give you hope when you need it most

If we had met even yesterday
In this imperfect world
Would we have learned to fly?
If I could tell you how I feel
I'd surely tell you every day
As long as I'm alive

It's a perfect night to walk out
Beneath the stars and the moon up so high
It's a perfect night to dream
Of you, and I'll tell you why
There's a kind of magic
That sits
In your eyes
And my heart starts to melt
Each time I
See you smile
If I could make
My dream come true
Then you would be
Here with me
Right now
My love
Well I live near the sea so it's perfect
To set the scene for a dream of you
Dancing across the sand barefoot while
The breeze it plays with your hair
There's a kind of magic
That sits
In your eyes
And my heart starts to melt
Each time I
See you smile
If I could make
My dream come true
Then you would be
Here with me
Right now
My love

A single tear

Of happiness

Makes my heart

A beat miss

It's like a diamond

In your eye

Please tell me I'm

The reason why

Each time I see a rainbow,
Or a butterfly

They remind me of certain things

Though I could not say the why

For all my pasts now blur

Into a long forgotten nightmare

Because when you hold my hand

At last I'm going somewhere

'Twas within the depths

Of my darkest winter

That you appeared to me

As the Goddess of my spring

Within a vision

Of you sleeping

Dreaming of summers

Yet to come

That first night I watched you sleeping

Upon some distant shore

Where your graceful symmetry

Set a storm raging through my core

Then with trembling heart I knew

Far beyond my fears and doubts

That now we were together

Life could no longer shut me out

A sigh as gentle as the mist
Came on the evening breeze
And whispered of what might come
If you were here with me
Motionless, entranced, stood I
Spellbound by all that I could see
Wondering if this was a dream
Brought on by thoughts of thee
Then, as the night drew in,
A single rose did flower
Glorious in the moonlight
Resplendent in its power
Tears fell from the sky
In a light, most delicate, shower
Yet not a cloud was present
Such was the magic of the hour

I have a photograph of you

Stood beneath a willow tree

Smiling, with your arms flung wide

As you called to me

And tho' 'tis but a simple thing

Just a memory

'Tis a wonderful reminder

Of how much you mean to me

Thou art the midsummer night's dream
That doth so make mine own heart race
Spellbound by thy beauty
And also by thyne grace
Thyne laughter is a clear blue sky
That doth mine spirit raise
And frees it from the memories
Of those darker days
Thyne eyes are limpid pools
In which mine soul reflects
Upon how fortunate I am
To thy love detect
Thyne hand's touch is as delicate
As the wings of a butterfly
Yet can bring me to my knees
And thou art the reason why
Thou art the midsummer night's dream
That doth so make mine own heart race
Spellbound by thy beauty
And also by thyne grace

Raindrops raced upon
The window pane
Shadows danced
By candle's flame
I held you,
In my heart
As on that path
We did embark
And in that moment
Of epiphany
I knew
That we had found
Our destiny

My Willow Lady come to me
And sing your song of what's to be
Of the past lives we once shared
Before Fate she so declared
That we must part in one world
Until we found ourselves again
And until then
We must live
In sorrow

So my Willow Lady come to me
And let us share what we can see
Of what for us the future may hold
As the years ahead unfold
For now we've found each other
We must not part again
Let it be said
For we no longer need
To live in sorrow

I'd love to be a part of your story
Give me a role and you won't be sorry
Because I believe in you
So why not take a chance
On me and romance
For soon we could be dancing

I'd love to be a part of your story
Give me a role and you won't be sorry
Because I'm in love with you
And if you take a chance
We could learn to dance
And soon we could be laughing

I'd love to be a part of your story
Give me a role and you won't be sorry
Because I'll always be here for you
So why not take a chance
On me and romance
For to me you are entrancing

I wished upon a shooting star
And you appeared - tho' from afar
To take me gently by the hand
And lead me to our promised land
Where by a stream, and willow tree
You did to me then reveal
That we could live a life sublime
Unheeding of the sands of time

I wished upon a shooting star
To be there now - tho' there is far
But distance is merely a trick of the eye
For in your arms I learned to fly
Beyond the dreams I dream once more
To find you on that distant shore
Where whether by night, or even day
I hope that there, with you, I'll stay

Moonlit night
With soul afire
To be with you
I do aspire
Waiting for
The light of dawn
To reveal my Goddess
Of the morn'

I have a secret in my heart
It is beautiful and fair
Soon I must reveal it
To show how much I care

That secret is no burden
For it sits lightly in my heart
Though it calls her name
And mourns when we are apart

My secret is both sun and moon
And all the stars combined
Mysterious, and powerful
She is graceful and refined

The secret in my heart
Was placed there by my Lady
Who bids me bide my time
Until the Fates are ready

Yet the secret in my heart
Calls out all the more
For the world to hear its voice
As our spirits soar

When will I meet
My Vision in Blue?
All I have
Is a photo of you
When will I meet
My Vision in Blue?

I'm a penniless poet
With nothing in my pocket
But you can have my heart
It's yours if you want it
For you are
My Vision in Blue

Tell me that
I'm your vision too
Anything you want
I'm happy to do
Tell me that
I'm your Vision in Blue

I searched for you
Through mists and clouds
I looked for your face
In every crowd
I dreamed of you
As sleep allowed
To find you was
My intent avowed
I heard your song
In the leaves of the trees
I heard your voice
On the waves of the sea
I felt your breath
On each gentle breeze
And I begged of Fate
Let me find you please

*Would you be
At all surprised
That when I look
Into your eyes
I find that deep
Within your gaze
A love to last us
All our days*

To while away
A passing hour
I picked the petals
From a flower
Then watched a cloud
That drifting by
Seemed to whisper
With a sigh
Your name with some
Angelic voice
And that is when
I made my choice
For what I have-
All I can do-
Is show my heart
Belongs to you

Despite all that I have been thru'
Despite all of life's travails
You make them seem so insignificant
You more than balance up the scales
For now we are together
How you make me strive
To let the whole world know
I'm the luckiest man alive

Sitting on the sea-wall
Watching the boats out in the bay
Dazzled by the sunlight
Reflecting on the waves
It reminded me of you
And your blue eyes oh so fair
Of your amazing lips
And your flowing hair
So I spent my day there
Thinking about you
Of how to me you're wonderful
And of all the things you do

My Lady
I've been thinking so much
About you lately
Of all about your charms
Of when you're in my arms
Of how when we're talking quietly
How you make everything seem new
So if you're ever feeling lonely
Or even feeling blue
Please try to remember
I love you

Just to hold your hand, it brings me joy
For you have healed my heart
And so in this life and the next
Say we'll never part

If there are any Gods
Who can see you and me
I ask of them to let us be
Together eternally

To me you are a rainbow
The laughter in my rain
To me you are the one
Who frees me from my pain

Your lips, so red, they fill me with desire
Your eyes they light in me a never-ending fire
Your arms around me make my heart begin to race
And I love it when you kiss me
And your hair brushes my face.

To wake beside you
Every morning
To see you stir
To the day that's calling
To see you begin to smile
To hear you speak my name
To know that you're the one
Who will never cause me pain
I pray that when you see me
That you feel the same

You are to me
A poem
That is so beautiful
To read
And how I love the fact
That each time I read
Your words
You remain
A mystery
For I dream of you
Even when
Awake
And I thank my lucky stars
For this act
Of Fate

Walk with me through fields
And down those winding lanes
Walk with me in sunshine
And with me in the rain
Walk with me forever
For on my heart you have a claim
Tell me that you love me
And I will do the same

I am yours
You are mine
Together now
For all time
All my strength
It comes from you
Without your love
What would I do?

I dreamed you were a flower
And I a buzzing bee
That flew across the fields
As you called to me
Enchanted by your scent
Dazzled by your beauty
To show to you my love
Clearly was my duty
You wrapped me in your petals
I whispered in your ear
Let us stay together
For I hold you dear

Let me be the one with whom
You would a new life start
Let me be the one
Who heals your broken heart

Let me be the one with whom
You share what you delights
Let me be the one
Who keeps you warm at night

Let me be the one with whom
You would wish to dance
Let me be the one with whom
You would dare to take a chance

Let me be the one with whom
You discover a new world
Let me be the one
Who sees your soul unfurl

Incredible and beautiful
And so much very more
Is it any wonder that
You're the one who I adore?

Gentle as a butterfly's wing

Your kiss does make my heart so sing

I think of you each night and day

Of all the joys you bring

You, my Lady, are my joy
Beyond compare you are
Of all that I could ask of life
I've found in you, and more
You make my soul feel lighter
When I see you smile
Everything about you
Makes my world worthwhile

To celebrate
All you've done for me
And how you make me feel
Would take forever and a day
All I hope and wish for
Is that you feel the same way

Meeting you
Was like feeling
The first drops of
Of a summer rain
It was like hearing music
For the first time
And realising
What I'd missed

In the midst of
My darkest night
You took my hand
And gave my light
For when I fell-
Just could not cope
You raised me up
And gave me hope

I met you in a mountain forest
Deep within a dream
Where we sat beside
A gently flowing stream
With a fire burning
To light us through the night
As we held each other
And watched the stars above so bright

It took you seconds
To find in me
What I thought
Had been lost
Forever

In the cutest way
You drive me insane
Lighting up my life
Like a golden flame

I loved you in a past life
I love you as much today
I will love you come tomorrow
And I will always say
That you are the star
Around which my world revolves
For every passing second
Sees my love for you evolve

You made our evening fantastic
We wined and dined and danced
As the hours flew by
By you I was entranced
And when we woke up in the morning
I could not believe my luck
As you stood there asking
Would I like to
Have breakfast?

*In our dreams
We had already lived
Our life together
Long before
We'd even
Met*

As I wandered through a desert
I came across a flower
Vibrant, full of life
Amazing in its power
Unable to go further
I had to stop and stare
For all that mattered to me
Was the flower that was there
Hypnotised, enchanted,
Spellbound by its beauty
I could only listen
As the flower then sang to me
Of a lonely soul
That wandered to and fro
Searching for a place
That it could call a home
And for that single flower
I began to care
I held it safe within my heart
For it was wonderful and fair
That desert was my life
And the flower it was you
And because of your song
My world began anew

A trace
Of your perfume
Dancing in the air
Sends my senses reeling
Even though you're
No longer there

Share with me this night
And each-other's charms
Let us fall asleep
In one another's arms
Let us be as one
And dream the world away
Let us search together
And together let us stay

Trembling
I placed my heart
In your hands
For I was weak
In your presence
Yet, somehow
You had made me
Feel
Stronger than
I could ever
Have
Imagined

In the mountains
Of my soul
In the valleys
Of my heart
Thoughts of you
Do linger there
Never to
Depart

Waking to the Light
Of you, my Morning Star
Tells me that together
We will journey far
Far beyond
The day's travails
To where the spark
Of Love prevails
Waking to the Light
Of you, my Morning Star
Tells me that together
We will journey far

Fate carved our names
Upon a tree
To be found
By you and me
For even then
As you can see
Fate knew you
Were meant for me

That then I watched you dancing
'Neath the silvered moon that night
Took my breath away
And set my soul alight
For in that forest deep
With our camp fire burning high
My heart began to melt
And I could only sigh
For then I knew I loved you
Without a hint of doubt
And the fire you lit within me
Could never then burn out

I always dreamed of meeting
Someone just like you
But was always terrified that
The wrong thing I'd say or do
But it didn't stop me
For I dreamed then all the more
That one day with some flowers
I'd be a knocking on your door
And that smiling you would greet me
Making me relax
Knowing that from that point
There'd be no turning back
Yet even it that dream
Is a hopeless fantasy
I can only hope
That you dream the same as me

Your touch is gentle as a sigh
And in your arms I'd gladly die
The joy to me your kiss does bring
Makes my soul so sing

Let me to you my love prove
So perhaps I can then your heart move
For you I would do anything
Be my queen, I'll be your king

When I'm with you time does so fly
I know the reason, I know why
For you make my heart miss a beat
With your beauty oh so sweet

Your auburn hair
Has a hint of red
That speaks of hidden fires
Your eyes shine
With the deepest blue
That speaks of knowledge higher
Your lips
So full and wonderful
Fill me with desire
Your mind
So sharp and crystal clear
Tells me you are wiser
So to my love
I lend my voice
For truth be told
I have no choice

I dreamed of an Elven princess
Dancing in a forest glade
Warmed by the autumn sun
Watered by its rain
And as she stepped so lightly
To some secret tune
I wondered if the dance changed
With the rising of the moon
Yet to me she seemed no stranger
'Twas as if I knew her well
And motionless I stood there
Afraid to break the spell
Until she at last saw me
And beckoned merrily-
No need to stand there lonely
Come join in with me-
So then thus invited
I made to hold her hand
But then the dream it ended
And I came to understand
That you were the princess
Laying by my side
And so I kissed you softly
As you gently sighed

I will be a fool for you
Just to make you smile
I will never be the reason
That you had to cry
I will try to be the one
Who makes you want to sing
I will be the one
Who to you flowers brings
I will be the one
Who wipes away your tears
I will be the one
Who soothes away your fears
I will be the one
And everything and more
If you will be the one
Who calls me to the fore

From my nightmares
Dark and deep
You save me when
I go to sleep
And because your love
To me is sweet
I give to you
My heart to keep

I could compare you to
A Chrysanthemum,
But
It's a tough one for me to spell
I even thought about
A Bougainvillea,
But
That's an awkward one as well
I considered being just like Shakespeare
And thinking of a rose,
But
Down that road, it seems, everybody goes
So I settled on a flower
That always makes me smile
A daisy, because it's cute,
And it reminds me of your nose

With ink on paper
I compose my thoughts
And thus I bare
My soul to you
To proclaim my love
And tell of hope
That you, my Lady,
Will feel too
As of me
As I of you

In a daydream I saw
The look in your eyes
Felt the warmth of your lips
'Neath the clear blue skies
The day passed into evening
And thence came the moonlight
As you kept me warm
Throughout the night

I wish that I could watch
The breeze play with your hair
But I'm left waiting here
And you are waiting there
If only we could find
A way to change our fate
And then get to meet
Before it is too late

I find myself
Thinking
In those silent
Hours
Deep within the crawl
Of night
How empty the world
Would be
Without
You

Dreaming
I may be only dreaming
What if my head's in the clouds
You know?
It's you of whom I'm dreaming
You're the reason that I'm dreaming
So let's get together
And go
There's a world
That's brand new
Waiting there
Waiting there just
For me and you
Dreaming
I may be only dreaming
What if my head's in the clouds
You know?
It's you of whom I'm dreaming
You're the reason that I'm dreaming
So let's get together
And go
Hold tight
Sit back and enjoy the ride
For too long
We've let life
Go passing by
Dreaming
I may be only dreaming
What if my head's in the clouds
You know?
It's you of whom I'm dreaming
You're the reason that I'm dreaming
So let's get together
And go

'What can you give me
That I don't already have?'
Is the strangest question
And it makes me sad
Because all I have to offer
Is my heart and soul
And for you they are both waiting
As surely you must know

'Tis a point
I must concede
For 'tis true
My heart does bleed
Since you sowed in me
True love's golden seed
'Tis a point
I must concede
For you, alone
Are all I need
I have no choice, I must obey,
To what Fate has decreed

You, my love,
Are beautiful indeed
And of your heady scent
How I love to breathe
So very far beyond
All my hopes and dreams
How can I not then wonder
What do you see in me?
Can I really so deserve
For you to think of 'us' as 'we'?
So I will spend my days
And I will spend my nights
Doing all I can
So I can prove you right

'Twould be madness
To deny
I will love you 'till
The day I die
And even then
With what may come next
I will still love you
I suspect

It wasn't hard
To then decide
To be forever
By your side
All it took
Was just one kiss
To know the chance
I could not miss
And so without
Further ado
I do proclaim
My love for you

There is nothing
I will not do
To prove that I'm
The one for you
Across broken glass
I'd barefoot walk
Just to hear you
When you talk
Across a desert
I would trek
To comfort you
When you're upset
Climb Mountain steep
Swim Ocean wide
Just to be
There by your side

I would love
To sit on the beach
With you as the waves
Our feet did reach
To watch the sunlight
On the sea
Together just sitting
Talking quietly

The pebbles in the stream
Have a lesson they can teach
For if you want to grasp one
Even if it's out of reach
You stretch yourself, if needs be,
Though it may seem a task
And it is the same
With the matters of the heart
For even if there's a risk
Of into the water falling
The thought of just not trying
Is simply just appalling
And so, needs must,
I must apply
Myself to
My heart's desire
For to win your love
I must try
And it is a case
Of do or die

If Fate could to me
One gift bring
It would to hear you
Once more sing
For your voice, to me,
Was the sweetest thing
And so to hope
I still do cling

A wishing well
In forest dell
To it my secrets
I do tell
Of how I wish
To be with you
Of how I wish
You'd love me too
I whisper to it
My hopes unseen
Every night
Within a dream

How I'd missed you
Through that day
As across the skies
Clouds did play
The rain did fall
From morn till noon
Until the sun
Began to bloom
Then a rainbow flew
Into my mind
Dispelling the gloom
It did there find
As across my face
There spread a smile
For you I'd see
In just a while

There is no-one
Across the land
Who could begin
To understand
How to me it feels
To hold your hand

There are castles in the skies
Floating past my mind's eye
Whether there by chance
Or by design
Of you, my love
They do remind
And you I never
Will forget
For to lose you
Would be
My life's regret

I'm not that much to look at
Most people would agree
And it's true that there are times
I don't act so sensibly
But for you, my Lady
I wear my heart upon my sleeve
For my love for you is true
As I hope you will believe
So please stay with me forever
Say you'll never leave

Walking through a field
Of dandelions and daisies
Upon a summer's day
The air was hot and hazy
So very high above
Was the promise of a storm
Within those rolling clouds
Thunder would be born
And so we walked on further
Happy and carefree
Until the rain was falling
And we took shelter 'neath a tree
There did we stand laughing
In each other's arms
And soon we were exploring
One another's charms
Then, when the storm was over
And the rain had ceased at last
We left the shelter of our tree
And walked back across the grass

If
I could
Do
But one thing
For you
It would be
To
Help
You to
Remember
All
Those things
That make
You
So
Special

Come with me and walk
Over hill, through dale
Beneath the autumn skies
With the sunlight turning pale
Come with me and find a place
That we may call our own
Come with me and find a place
Where the seeds of love are sown

Let's dream together
Throughout the night
And dream even more
Come the morning light
Let's dream of the life
We'll have together
Through the good times and bad
No matter the weather
For together we can
Each other joys bring
For together we can
Do anything

My Lady,
You are like a flower
Growing sweeter
By the hour
How I love
Your divine scent
To me you seem
From Heaven sent

Watching you
As you slowly wake
To the morning light
Is
One of the greatest joys
I could
Ever
Have

A fearsome, fatal, symmetry
Revealed by candle light
That in our darkened room
Show your eyes so bright
Slick with perspiration
Limbs fluid, yet entwined
While the seconds lose all meaning
As does the sense of time
And gently urging sighs
Demanding in intention
Call on forces far beyond
Mere physical invention
In that act of joining
As old as moon and sun
When two souls become
No longer two but one

In our arms the secret divine
What I have is yours as yours is mine
Though not in haste
Still eager to taste
Each other's minds,
Bodies
And souls

Lead me into passions
Frenzied and sublime
Let us reach the heights
Of ecstasy each time
Let our cries of pleasure
Come from our very essence
As we come together
Calling down the heavens

That first time
We came together
Like storm tossed waves
Crashing against
A rock strewn beach
And there
In the throes
Of our glory
We shattered
Entire worlds

The whole of our philosophy
Revealed its very core
As we lay together
Upon that mossy floor
And as the moonlight speckled
Its path down through the trees
The world surrounding us
Simply ceased to be

D W Storer

D W Storer is a multi published author whose works range through the occult, children's books, and organic philosophy, Currently residing in Exmouth, Devon, he lives in dreams and dreams of living- if you ever find yourself in Exmouth feel free to look him up and have a chat

All of D W Storer's works can be found on Amazon
Any enquiries / suggestions can be sent direct
To the author via Facebook
facebook.com/dwstorerauthor

The Key of the Storm raises the curtains on the darkly provocative trilogy, Through the Mirror Darkly.

Comforted by a powerful mystic as he observes the grisly conclusion to his death, DW Storer's autobiographical antihero is taken on a journey of classical proportions, as he absorbs, celebrates, and ultimately confronts lessons learned during the dawning of his afterlife.

Set in a timeless astral plane that is home to an exotic array of gods, kings, queens, ferocious beasts, historical figures and tortured souls, Storer includes factual accounts of his spiritual development and encounters with entities, both benign and malevolent, to reinforce his central tenet that even the most finely tuned will is susceptible to otherworldly temptation.

re-edited with new poetry, Poems Without A Home is a journey through the darkness of depression, madness, epiphany, and coming to terms with mortality - paganesque , Luciferian , philosophical, it will walk you through the shadows and into the darkness beyond before you find the answers to questions that far too many are afraid to ask

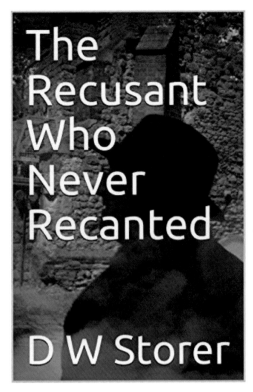

this is the 3rd book in the Through the Mirror Darkly series - and continues the story began in The Key of The Storm -formed of two parts - part 1, The Child Who Died of Other Tales the anti-hero returns to guide his former mentor through a prequel journey – part 2 -The Recusant Who Never Recanted sees the Storm tempt the Celt with the opportunity to pass judgement on those perceived to be evil - yet to do so would save few in the attempt to create a more just world. D W Storer's unique style of antique prose and dark poetry takes the reader back into uncharted territory where a subtle venom questions and tests all faiths, beliefs, and moralities even at the very end

Ever wondered about where the years have gone? Getting older? Search your memories with this collection of poems that ask the questions we all need to ask - how did I get here and what happened on the way?

With only seven sleeps 'till Christmas Blue Ted is too excited to sleep - find out how Bedtime Bear helps him - easy to follow poetry with simple rhymes - sure to delight your child as you read along with them

Hidden Easter Eggs ! What's a Teddy Bear to do? Especially one that's tiny, furry, and is blue. More of Blue Ted's adventures, including train rides, rainy days, and surprises galore that small children and their parents will surely then adore

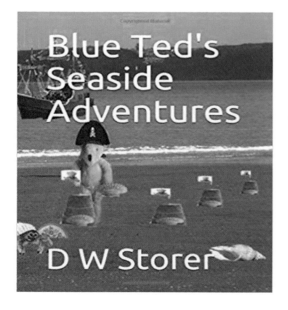

A trip to the seaside, a trip to the zoo - and all of the things for a small Teddy to do. Join in with your child and Blue Ted on treasure hunts and all sorts of fun- easy to read rhymes, it's sure to keep the little ones happy

Blue Ted's Adventures continue with a Halloween party, fireworks, games, and the chance to meet some of his friends too! A big Hello from Blue Ted - to me, and them, and you. To tell you all of his adventures is what we're here to do- and you'll get to meet some of his special friends -with something new each day the fun will never end

Snow filled fun for our furry friend. Snowmen, snowballs, and more. The fun it seems to never end with Blue Ted's tales galore

Book 7 in the Blue Ted Adventure series- Join Blue Ted on his Viking quest as he goes in search of treasure and to defeat a dragon- but is everything as it seems? Across the sea and far away our friend Blue Ted must go -but will he survive and win the day? Read on if you would know. Talking walruses, flying fish, magic books, a lettuce, and even a Viking who gets to fly to the moon!

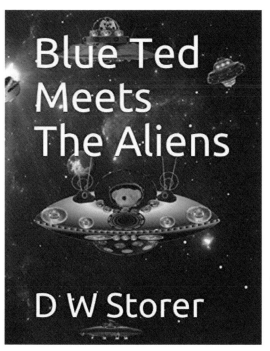

Blue Ted's adventures have taken him to outer space. But he's not gone for long, nor without a trace. Aliens, spaceships, robots, and more in these tales you will adore. Furrily going where no Bear has gone before Blue ted's adventures take him on a trip into outer-space where he meets an alien who needs his help to get back home. To save his new friend Blue Ted has to work his way through some of the strangest situations he's come across yet!

From the Blue Ted's Adventures series - meet Grunkle the Turd Fairy! Turd Fairies and bottom burps - Hippos and dinosaurs - Greedy children eating slugs- and of course there's more! Every page has something new- full to the brim with surprises for you - So now you know what you must do - buy a book that's full of poo!

36859685R00068

Printed in Poland
by Amazon Fulfillment
Poland Sp. z o.o., Wrocław